A Twin Is to Hug

By Boni Ashburn · Illustrated by John Nez

ABRAMS BOOKS FOR YOUNG READERS · NEW YORK

A twin is a mirror who looks just like you.

Or maybe you're different.

But still, there are two.

Maybe same nose or similar eyes.

Maybe same giggle!

Maybe same cries.

A twin is two tummies!

Four ears.

Twenty toes.

Two moods . . .
attitudes . . .

and a bond that
just grows.

A duet.

A matched set.

Always two—never more.

A twin is a shadow who's hard to ignore.

A twin is a nudge.

A gesture.

A look.

A twin lap is just
the right size
for a book.

A twin is enough to play follow-the-leader.

A twin is your
food-I-don't-want-to-eat eater!

A twin is a whisper.
A partner
in crime.

A twin is an echo.
A mimic.
A rhyme.

A twin can go first.

But a twin has to share.

Everything.

Always.

And no, it's not fair.

A twin must take turns.

A twin has to wait.

A twin will compare,
and compete,
and debate.

A twin is to hug.

Or to kiss!

Or to shove.

It's all about balance.

It's all about love.

Whatever the weather, a twin is together.

A rock to your roll.

A heart to your soul.

A twin is a language
you both understand.

A twin is your *also*, your *too*,
and your *and*.

Hand in hand, side by side,

a twin is your friend.

Every step of the way,

from beginning to end.

For Jack and Lily, who even have to
share this dedication —B. A.

For brothers and sisters of every kind —J. N.

The illustrations in this book were done with a pencil, paper,
an eraser, imagination, and Photoshop.

Cataloging-in-Publication Data has been applied for and may
be obtained from the Library of Congress.

ISBN 978-1-4197-3158-7

Text copyright © 2019 Boni Ashburn
Illustrations copyright © 2019 John Nez
Book design by Julia Marvel

Printed and bound in China
10 9 8 7 6 5 4 3 2 1

Abrams Books for Young Readers are available at special discounts when
purchased in quantity for premiums and promotions as well as fundraising or
educational use. Special editions can also be created to specification.
For details, contact specialsales@abramsbooks.com or the address below.

Abrams® is a registered trademark of Harry N. Abrams, Inc.

ABRAMS The Art of Books
195 Broadway, New York, NY 10007
abramsbooks.com